White
Man
Book

Robin Wyatt Dunn

ISBN: 978-1-940830-12-4
Library of Congress Number: 2016905861

Published by John Ott
San Diego, California

for all the rebels

I.
Crazy
White
Man

White man, he write book. Good thing! No two alike. No book like white man book. Strong book. Big book. White book.

White man, he write the book. He know book. Book write him too. No book like book. No book at all like White Man Book. Good. Good book. He write it.

No book like white man book, but he know, other books too. You don't need other books. Need white man book. Good book. White man book.

You can read book, you anybody. Anybody, book. Read.

Read book, good. Good. Book read you too.

What I want to tell you is: this book good. This book white too. That's okay. White is okay too. Just crazy, white. We crazy. That's why we funny. Crazy funny. Crazy white man, he write the book. And the book say, "okay, write me then."

So I do.

Nobody knows white man. He ethnic like that. He is special. Nobody like him. Other people, they special their own way. Not like him. He special in white man way. He know the white man things.

White man think: these things, they may exist. Why not write down?

So he do.

What do he know, you ask?

He know how to be a white man.

Everybody interested now: white man this, white man that. This man, he white. This other man, he ain't white. Or maybe he white and maybe he ain't.

I here to tell you: I white. I know it.

How do I know?

I know.

Maybe that don't mean nothing. Maybe it do mean something. But what I say is: it must mean something, because everybody know it mean something.

You can't not be white and not know it. You can't be white and not know it either.

I know it: I white.

This book be mine, no matter what you say. I write it. Is my book. Not your book. Is mine.

You write whatever book you want. This one

mine.

I come from a place, high in the mountains. So far away, you would not even believe. You would not even believe this place. It is ethnic place. It is so ethnic, that it is special. This is why he love his home, even though he just a baby when there.

No one else knows the place he from. It is his own. Place is not white, he white.

Where is the white place? He not know this.

In time, he move away.

Now he here.

Big town. Big man. Big book.

I know, you might be saying. This book racist. Or, as they know in overseas, racialist. It is, this racist book. Because is white book. How can you not be white and be racist? I know. Maybe.

What do you think?

I know, I know already. You think: man hates everybody. Because he white. He even hate the other white people.

Or maybe you think: this man just jealous of the black people. You right.

My book not big and special. It not go around the world. It small and stupid, like me.

Book not matter, really. Not even a Big White Book. That is okay. Who care about book? They only these things we carry round. Like detergent.

One time, I got a book. Bunnicula, it called. Little rabbit, he drink blood. White skin, need blood to live. He drink carrot juice, and other things. Wampyr rabbito! Man alive what a bunny.

This book was in a school. I know, so what? Well, I'm telling you. This school, you buy books. Not school books. Fun books. Then, the people, they get money, and you, you get a book.

Capitalism.

Then I leave that place. No good no more. Got to go West.

I cun hear what I know; it inside me. Where, I dunno. Could be mine, or yours. Not really a white book, not when you get inside. But is mine.

We know this. I sorry for the trouble. Okay, is not white book. Just a book. Maybe a White Book, but not a white book. Is not matter anyway.

The story matter. Or maybe not! Hahaha.

What do you think you get from the story? The truth? Hahahaha

Lies? Hahahahah

Maybe all at once? Yeah. Good thing too. We know what you need. We might give it to you too, if you got the money.

You got the money, white man? Black woman? We don't care the color of you money, just that you got some. Yuan? Chang Kai Shek? Rope a dope fun ball amulets? These are acceptable. All currencies are the currency of god!

You want book? You pay.

Here now, you pay yet? You pay, go on. Pay up.

Is good book. Give me money, or the man here, he can take it, and give some to me.

Pay him!

Yes. Good. This book, you can keep it.

The book, it is yours now. I write it, but now you write it too.

Yes, at the beginning, I was a smurf. In Gargamel's mansion. I was his kin, Jewish maybe, or is he a Gypsy? Not sure. Ethnic, though. Real Romanian gypsy. Magic spell, magic cat, eating little blue people. Romania.

I am kin to him, in the long span of the whirling ball, and maybe he know me . . . no. He can't know me. He Gargamel. But I love him.

You know Gargamel? No? Let me tell you bout him. He big and strong. Curvy like an old Jew. Old tinker Jew, big wart on his big nose, crazy look in his eye. Lives in a shack in the woods, super ethnic! He loves Smurfs. He wants to eat them. The mushroom people.

This Gargamel, he shaman.

From sramana, that be Sanskrit. Mean worker. Worker bee. He be worker.

Working on the mushroom people.

Is good the children know him. Children love him. He Santa Claus, except more ethnic.

Santa, Gargamel, he loves you. He want to get you high.

Oh well. Why not?

White Man Book, he know where he go. Somewhere. Not like some books, one this way, then another way. This one know. It go one way. Up.

To god.

Yes, it simple.

Simple to say.

But to get to know god, you got to get to know reality first. This not so simple.

Who is he, Reality? What he know? What he want? How he get here?

We not sure. We goan find out.

What you know, Reality? You know man? Woman? Love?

And then what happen? What after man and woman? We not there yet.

Stay on what you know. Man, woman, baby.

White man know he important and afraid. He in suburbia.

Know all about the light.

What that light saying.

It saying: "shhhh, little baby. don't fret now. just wait."

We was waiting. Now, maybe we ain't waiting so much no more.

Some of you still saying: this white man, he racist. Or, racialist.

What is the difference? Hehehe

Okay, let me be racialist. Is okay. There are worse things. I never kill nobody.

Never even beat nobody up. Wanted to plenty of times. Bad, I know. I bad.

But we in suburbia, now, okay?

The houses are white.

People stay inside the houses.

I play with blocks.

What the difference?

I doan know. But something different.

This thing, it was there. Bad. Not bad dad, or bad mom.

Something in the light maybe. God. Maybe God know, what we did. He tell us: now you hide inside those houses. So we do.

They argue. Good mom, good dad. Then you go away. Move West.

White man come to Texas. Texas, he mean taysha, friends, in Caddo tongue. Hahaha.

Texas be friends.

Texas/ Taysha be word for this thing. Like irony. But not irony. Something deeper. God. No, that too deep. Something in between. Judgment. They do judgment, in that Caddo name. Like mad.

White man come to there, me. White boy.

White boy now white man still white boy.

There in Texas, there were black people and white people. Brown people didn't exist. They exist, but we pretend not.

White man is sorry. What does white man know? It was there, he was in it. Now it over.

Yes, it over now.

Make it be over, white man. Do Gargamel's magic, make it go way.

I do it. I do it now, white man. Make it all go away. Into my magic hat. Zazoom!

Paroom! It go bye bye.

No more grievances from yon place. No more worries.

Ha ha ha.

Yes, Texas is evil. Friends are evil. They are the worst.

Now white man, he say: sorry. We saying it, I know. Not enough of us, yet. We real sorry. Didn't know. Didn't know what we did. Did in our name. That's not right. Not our name. In our vengeance. What we did for vengeance. Vengeance for what, I doan know. For what? King George? No.

I don't know.

White man, he say: "we all one people now." Hmm. I'll think on that.

This racialist story, it about this white boy. He was a boy who knew poverty (hahahaha), and then he knew poverty again (hahaha) and later he went on a trip to Europe and went crazy. Not like to Ibiza and the rich man crazy.

He went poor man homeless crazy, screaming at skies. White man be crazy. White man be strong. He know reality is not sane. He just like reality.

White man is sorry he did those things. He

know was upsetting to nice folk. But nice folk, you get out of town. No room for you now.

We in Texas now. We know just what we do with friends: shoot em dead.

There was this white boy, in a Texas town. Good white boy, small, skinny. Readin them books. Playing on them video games. Playing with the other white boys, and black boys, and brown boys, who didn't exist.

Texas knew a lot about what didn't exist no mo, more than that mountain place in suburbia town. It knew how to Gargamel vanish-o the bad things and make them into good things. They did it every day in school.

You say it crazy, but it just Texas: walking wit our listen ears and our hand over our mouts, like good little Nazis, all the colors of the rainbow.

Obeying Austin.

Oh well. Austin is dead now. And we leave Texas behind. Bye bye Texas.

Hello, California.

White man, he know he good. He know he blessed by god. But what do this blessing by god mean? What can he do with his special power? Girls, they do not fall at his feet because of his special blessing. Nor do they undress spontaneously, in supermarkets, or in the classroom, or when he readin his book at home.

Some girls do undress in the girly magazine, but these girls be different. They don't have girls like them at school.

White man does not know what to do. What are these girls? What do they want? We haven't figured that one out yet.

Is mystery, you know? Like god. No, not like god. Like cheeseburgers. A cheeseburger is a mystery. So is girl.

White man, he know it is hard. He know not everyone like him. He know he safe. He know he know everything he need to know. Except he don't.

What do he not know? Where he at. Who he be. Why he be doin the things he be doin.

We can say, well, now we know. But we don't. Not really. We only guessing.

I guessing now: I say, well that white man, young white man, he was schemin. Tryin to fine his way out. Like Malcolm X. Thinking of a good way to kill himself some motherfuckers, without getting no blame on him.

White boy, he get himself a friend. Name Roam Mirandian. This a made up name you understand. He got this other name. This a fictional character we talking about. No relation to the actual one.

This Roam character, he real skinny, real up on them girls. He rich white man. Real skinny, real good with them girls. Except he don't know how to talk to them yet, because he always reading books. Like the white man is. So they friends now.

Go out places together, no lookin at girls, just talkin. They don't do much. Just look around. Try to prove who's better.

"I am the best white man!" opines Roam Mirandian.

"No, I be the best white man," opines myself.

We go on in this way.

Later, Roam Mirandian proved he was the best white man when he was hired by Microsoft Corporation and work on the Bing.

These days, Roam is a successful white man. Not like myself. Roam, he know that White Men do not exist no more, and that this is a Great Blessing. Myself, is not so sure about this. For instance, I still believe I exist, but I am not sure why.

White man, he know how to get drunk. He been workin at it. I too know this. Even last night, I was drunk. We know it. White man, he know the liquor has the spirit. The spirit of god. We find it. Then it go away. Maybe later, we find it again.

Now, with White Man and the Liquor, we know it a problem. Same way God is a problem. What to do? We don't know.

I am a white man now, and I am living in the West. We know it is a good thing, because we often say so. All the people know this, people of black persuasion, and brown. Yellow people do not know this. They were East already, so what is West? Hardly even exist.

I want to know, what is it? I may find out.

Does the White Man still exist? Yes, he do. Does the white man still say he exist? Yes, he often do.

Now, why do the white man say he still exist? Is it he afraid he do not? Yes, that is reason. White man be afraid. Of all those ghosts. This is why he drink.

When White man was a boy, he was enrolled in school. This taught him to be silent, and quiet. Also very still. He is still this way. But sometimes he moves around some.

The white man knows that movement is dangerous. This is why he either moves not at all or he moves furiously, without stopping. Move just a little and you might get shot.

This racialist story. Who be the different races? Who be the ones who are not any races? Where are you roots.

All got the different roots and the same roots. Mine and yours. I don't know why it is. We must talk about it, though. Otherwise we are shot.

Some of my roots, they are in that England place. This England place, it was brown people, then later, white people.

Before that, just mammoths. (And snow). Before that, dinosaurs.

We know we are not dinosaurs. We like to eat them.

The different races, they are confused.

But white man, he say he is not confused. He say, everythin make sense.

I too. I say: this do not make any sense. This makes sense.

Racialist story, it look down at the ground. Of what dirt are you composed of? Is the question.

It was that England place for White Man. What one of those tricky brown writers says: place of bog people. I like that tricky brown writer. He may be right. Bog dwellers.

I don't know. If I knew all the history, I would not know.

Now here in my city, we know all about it. Roots are something you forget about every day, and remember every night.

During the day, they get in the way. During the night, they are everything that you are.

People feel sorry for the White Man now. But why not for the Black Man? The reason is: the Black Man is scarier than the White Man. He has to be. He is still outnumbered by a small margin. But maybe numbers is not the reason.

Maybe the reason is: the White Man merely longs to be as scary as the Black Man, but he will never be this. He gave up being scary when he turned white.

This White Man Book is a good thing. I will say no more about it.

Now, people be saying: Reparations. Let the White Man pay up. I agree with this. I know some White Men and they have money. Also there are some Black Men with money. Money repairs many things.

What is our wer geld, our man-money? Put a price on our heads. Then we will be atoned.

Here in the White Man Book, all is clear as day.

Punish the White Man, because he is good no longer. Possibly, in the future, he will be good again. But for now, he is in prison.

This is all right. In prison, one can write books, like Malcolm X.

Good racialist books. Who see where we go.

Once upon a time, all the races, they live together, the Bible tell us. Then God, he angry. At what, we don't know. Then he make us all different.

Why God do it, we don't know. That is, we know he punish us, but we not know why.

What do the punishment mean? It mean we angry. We angry like god. We different like god.

Angry White Man, he be angry. He make White Man Book. He know it stupid. But it good. No one else will do it. So he do it. Why be angry, when you can be White Man Book Man? No reason.

Do the book help out?

Do the book make it better?

Do the book say: now do this.

Do the book say: now, it better this way.

Do the book say: I know the answer. It this.

Do the book say: we done figured it out.

All these books, trying. To find out. What happen to us.

Why God do it.

Letters be the handmaiden of theology. Just waitin around on the god word. Waiting to see if he ope his mouth and let out a big fart.

Pppppppptppptpptpptpptpthththtthtppthththhhhh

2.

White Man, He Make Big Journey

Now white man, he know he goin some place. Got brain in his head, and when he get to be fifteen, he get tall.

Now the girls see him. Tall white man. Stupid, but big. Sometimes they say hello to him. He nods and smiles back, because he is an idiot.

White man thinks he is going places. He is right; he is.

These are some of the places the white man has been.

"In jail I saw myself for the first time.

There was a man, he came up to me, and he said:

'Are you white?'"

"In the showers, there was great joy. It was the furthest from tension you could imagine, while the water was on.

"Then, a short brown woman with a whip came out, and turned on the gas. Some of the men cried.

"Later, we were obliged to bend over and show our anuses to the men in uniforms. They had discussions about the anuses of the men.

"Then, we were asked to raise our scrotums so that they could look under them.

" 'If you do not know how to raise your scrotum, look at the scrotum of the man next to you,' they said. Some men did."

In jail, they told White Man, "You go."

White Man was not good to be in jail. Too crazy.

White Man was knowin things not good to know. These ideas, they be bein in his head.

Other prisoners feel them.

White man not say a word. No good.

"You go," they say. So he go.

White Man is a monkey. He knows all about it. Inside, the monkey is waiting. Sometimes, he is not waiting. He is just being. You can open your mouth, and be a monkey. Make the monkey sounds.

This is what I did. It got me out of jail.

White Man Book be the record of the White

Man. Sometimes, the White Man has been going. Sometimes, the White Man has been stopped. Sometimes, he has not been sure as to which it was: going, or not. At these times, there is much debate.

"Where are we going?"

Politicians have opinions on the issue.

But the White Man Book knows the truth: we are not going anywhere. We are still here. Soon, some of us will go to Mars. But most of us will stay here.

The movie, The Graduate, no it was not the Graduate. The movie . . .. well it was a movie, with a man in it, Berton Stockholm. No, that wasn't his name. Well, this movie had a theory about the racialisms. Bernie Stockholm had the theory in this movie. The theory went like this:

"When we all fuck each other, racialism go away."

White Man good in English. He good. Write things down. Write more things down. Teacher say, good, write. Teacher look serious when he say it. Good, good.

Good, good. White man good. Know things. Write.

White man know to write. Not know anything else. But know this.

Write down. Make it go.

Make it go, and we go with you, maybe. Maybe we are going. No, we not, but let's pretend. Pretend we goin.

Okay: here we go.

I am a white man, and this is my story. There are many like it, but this is mine. Go be you. Or as the kids say nowadays, "you do you." Or as the black man who hired me for my first job said: "I be E.B., you be you." That was also his license plate. IBEBUBU.

I be white man, but what I want to know is: is this a real thing?

Yes, white man, it is.

Okay, but was it always a real thing?

Yes, white man, as soon as man turned white, it was real.

But why did he do this?

Because of wheat, white man. This is why the words sound the same. Wheat, white.

What of Malcolm X's theory on the origin of white men?

It was wheat.

Why did we eat it?

We had eaten all the animals. Had to eat something.

White man, he eat wheat.

This original lord's prayer.

But who was the original lord? A white man.

Before that, there were no lords. Only kings.

Why did we do it?

We kept making babies.

But I thought making babies was the solution

to White Man?

That is only Bernie Stockholm's theory. There are lots of theories in Hollywood.

Here in Hollywood, there are a few white men. Mostly there are people who are not white men. This is true in the world generally. White men are a minority population.

How did we get to be so ridiculously "successful"?

Well, this isn't a history book. But the history books won't tell you either. Some of the 19th century histories did. White man, he conquer winter! Then he conquer the world!

White man does not conquer Hollywood. Jews, they conquer Hollywood. Muslims, yes, them too. Arabs, yes. Russians, okay, fine.

White man, your theories do not hold. White Man no good theory. Make theory go bye bye. Stay close to White Man, white man. White Man will show you what it mean.

Inside the brain, White Man know things. This may also be the case for folk who not be White Men. White Man not know. What he know is: I know.

Here is what I know. Here I am. I white. Why is everything not perfect?

Why have the naked ladies and the money not shone down on me? Why is I the nigger baby, Mr. Baldwin? Why is it?

Well, someone has to be the nigger baby. Might as well be me.

White Man. Not sure who he is. Not sure who anyone else is. Not sure.

Is Mr. Baldwin right, that I be the nigger baby? Mr. Baldwin he be smarter than me, maybe he right. When someone the nigger baby, at least then we know: who it is.

If no one the nigger baby, how will we know, who is the nigger, and who is not?

This world peace stuff, it for the birds. Even god is against it!

White man, he get the water on his head. Not like they do down South, with the river and the prayin, this White Man, he Protestant, get the little sprinkle over his brown hair, then he blessed.

Clean of sin. Clean of thought.

Gots to be clean. Clean up good. Smile at the pretty girl, ask her to dance.

White man not clean no more.

No more bless, no more sinlessness.

Plenty of that upstairs action. Thought.

White man, he thinkin. He thinkin: what do I be?

This idea, White Man. Like a word made flesh. Keep talking about it, and it you be.

You are what you talk.

One day, I will no longer be a white man. This the day Martin Luther King saw in his dream. The writing was on the wall, Nebuchadnezzar and all the Super Friends said: the Justice League be comin, and we all be Americans soon, liberty and freedom for all the children of the world.

Good TV show, that one. They don't make em like that now. Now is the ethnic shows. For every ethnic, its own TV show.

What ethnic you be?

Well, I ain't sure.

Here, look at this list of channels.

White Man Channel.

White Man, is beer good?

Oog.

Books?

Oog oog.

What of the women?

Oog.

Here, for 29.99 we can sell you White Man Hat.

I wear it on the way to the supermarket.

The other day, a brown man wanted to sell me his hat. For one dollar. I already had White Man hat on my head. But this brown man wanted to sell me his hat, for a dollar. This was on the subway. He was a nice young man, and it was a nice straw hat. An amazing price, at a dollar. But on my head was already White Man Hat.

"No thank you," I said. The brown man smiled.

White Man Hat is floppy, with a string around

it so you can tie it to your chin. This prevents it blowing off your head in Los Angeles subway traffic.

You can say: this White Man Book is just Something That Happened.

And this is true. It is. White Man is solemn and respectful in the presence of Something that Happened. And the White Man Book knows it might be something like Whatever Happened. It won't be, but it's possible to imagine that it was.

You can say: well, it's over now. And it is. All white men know that it is all over.

What is it, to know it's over?

Maybe, like to know it was wrong to start with. That's usually how it is.

The girl, she gets to be annoying. And you think: I knew it, the girl was annoying. Why didn't I see it before?

So it is with white men. This violent race that keeps killing everyone else off. Why did we ever think they were charming?

We went crazy in the snow. That snow is so white. It's painfully white. Maybe, those ancestor white men of mine went so crazy that they just had to kill. To get rid of that painful blindness in the snow.

I know, this is no history book. White Man Book know no history, only what happens upstairs, and this be fine, yes, sho. I know, history barely even exists any more. It's all over now. It's an eternal present, like Mandarin Chinese. Still, maybe it existed once upon a time, even if it doesn't now.

White Man Book postulates:

What if it wasn't the snow?

What if it was Turkey? The same food we enjoy every Thanksgiving, except we're talking about the nation state of Turkey.

Unfortunately, White Man does not know any history. No one told White Man. And White Man too stupid to figure it out for hisself.

Still, might be Turkey.

In the Fertile Crescent of Los Angeles, White Man knows things. He knows things are good, but how does he know this?

What does it mean for "things" to be "good"?

For instance, once upon a time the Icelanders held a Thing and it was they government. In the England place, they still do this, but it is called Hus-things, where politician get on stage and make noises.

Ooog oog.

Do things be good?

Oog oog!

I want my Turkey.

I know, you is saying: White Man Crazy. No make sense!

You right.

3.
White Man, He Holy Bible

This White Man lives in California. And This White Man Book is actually my more-books-than-I-can-count-on-both-hands book. But it is the first book to be called White Man Book, after the Holy Bible, that is.

There is White Man Book, and then the Holy Bible, except in reverse, order, if you're talking about chronology, or that order, if you mean quality.

If you mean quality, try White Man Book. We don't know much, but we know White Men. And we even know there are other people out there! But we don't understand them.

The idea of white men basically originates in the following conundrum: people sure are different.

White Man knows different. Every white boy knows different. You got to be different to be a white boy, because if you became the same, that would be no good. That would be wrong!

In difference, we are safe. We are White. White even means good, in old fashioned terms. We don't say that any more though, just like we don't say the racialist words any more. It's good to get rid of things like White Men.

Spring Cleaning.

It's true, the problem of White Men is an identical problem to the problem of Modern Germany, a theory that the former Nazi and now dead German writer Gunter Grasse expressed perfectly as: "The 20th Century is the century that Germany fucked up royally."

Just like Modern Germany, White Men killed everyone they could get ahold of and eventually people became resentful of this.

In the case of Germany, we partitioned them, and later we warned them, you need to be real sorry.

In the case of White Men, we told them, recently mind you, "you're nothing special."

This was devastating news for White Men. If we're not anything special, what are we?

If we're not special, how can we even exist?

Although I am a White Man writing White Man Book, I can entertain theories that appear to attack the Weltanschauung of White Man. For instance, I believe it is possible to be white and to be nothing special.

However, if this were true, I would not be writing White Man Book. I would be an insurance agent or something.

I have a White Man friend, he became an insurance agent. I even saw a photo of him kneeling in the meadow with his inoffensive wife and children, grinning a huge Midwestern insurance agent's White Man grin.

This photo provokes a strong suicide in White Man.

On the one hand, this White Man in the Insurance Business in Midwestern America has succeeded in becoming nothing special by entering that Insurance Business in Midwestern America. But doesn't this mean he is not White any more?

He is smarter than me. He got over bein white, and concentrated on making money instead.

Me, I'm another story.

Which of us is Whiter?

Me. I'm special. And more ethnic. My experience is valuable. Because it is special.

Because of my ethnic poverty.

Yes, even whites have ethnic poverty.

And my eternal arrogance.

Like the arrogance of god.

Whiteness will not stop.

Once, I had a White Man Car and a White Man job and a White Man girlfriend and a White Man career. Then, I jettisoned all of those things and just concentrated on being a White Man without a car, job, girlfriend, or career.

This has been working out well.

What everybody knows about White Man Books today is that it is forbidden to do them. This is a good reason to do them.

Why?

It's fun.

Also, you learn things.

What are white people like?

It occurs to me that this book would sell better if it were Jew Book. But there is intense competition to write Jew Book and this frightens me. And I can't think of anyone writing White Man Book. There it is.

It's like the Wild West out here. An unconquered territory. Nor will my big White Man Book be enough to do so. Just a few shots in the dark, into this dark and infinite land of beauty.

Those who know White Man Book is no good are right. There's nothing good about it. Even though it be a good book. It be no good as a book.

As a thing, okay, something to hit people with, it's okay, you can use it.

I'm going to use it to hit you. I'm sorry.

It's okay. It's just a little love tap.

I know you're wondering: what is the difference between a Jew Book, a White Man Book, and a Black Man Book?

There is no difference. Or that's what we want to believe.

We want to believe there are no important differences.

And we may be right in believing that.

What is an important difference and what is an unimportant difference?

An important difference is one that has bearin on survival. An unimportant difference does not affect survival.

But what does and what does not affect survival?

What is a primary and what is a secondary sexual characteristic, for instance?

Well, bein big and strong is primary, and having a beard or big tits is secondary, supposedly. But beards and big tits can get the opposite sex to want to fuck you! That sounds pretty primary to me. What they're there for.

What, ultimately, is not about the bedroom?

We don't know what races could or could not mean any more than we know what nations could or could not mean. Except as ways to get each other into bed.

So, the Bullworth Solution (that's the movie, it was Bullworth, with Hamford Dinglestein), is right, except that fuckin each other doesn't end racism is just makes it more intense. It makes us ever more increasingly interested in shades of difference. The slightest amount. The fairest chance. The tenderest caress.

What is the difference between a Jew Book, a White Man Book, and a Black Man Book? Well, they're all in capitals. All very important. And the Jew Book should really read Jew Man Book, because most of them too, are about men. But not all of them!

And, I was trying to duck away from my antecedents. Notwithstanding the various racist creeds that have been published, there are still upstanding instances of the White Man Book that have been published before. White Fang, for instance. It be White too. But it is not concerned with the "ethnic" experience of it except insofar as it influences the "Westernness" of it. We think of it as a "Western" book and not a "White" book.

And, of course, with most of these books, of whatever color, we're really talking about Ruling Class Books. Rich people problems. First world problems. Even if you're a poor "third worlder," you're still supposed to talk about rich, first world problems.

Supposed to. Or you be shot.

This White Man Book is the truth. It is mine. I wrote it, and it is about a White Man. I am afraid. Corny. Abusive. Honest. Dishonest. A poet. Like Whitman. Another White Man. Like Ginsberg. A Jew Man. Men and their problems.

I wish I'd been born a Jew. Then I'd have a set of

culturally respected problems. My ancestors were oppressed, and I may well be too. Consistency. Resolution. Truth.

What of my ancestors? Howard Zinn knows they were just as oppressed, since most of us are the offspring of working people, with the occasional dash of "noble blood" thrown in there, for some frisson.

But how did the White People get it so real wrong?

People still want to be seen as white today. I still want to be seen as white today. It's important. We care. This stupid racist meme will not die. It can't die, not as long as we live.

But if Baldwin is right, and he be right, then everybody fighting to be the Real Nigger Baby. Be the Real Nigger Baby, so you can see, just what it means:

This White Man has been places, into the clouds, with the rest of you modern people, going to the places to see them, like Henry James, but at faster speed, to witness all that History they got over there in Europe. Even more of it in Africa but most Americans don't go there, unless it's to talk about Jesus.

Jesus he know Poor White Boy. Cause he was one, even if he was a Jew who didn't Actually Exist.

Jesus know just how it is. Jesus know you need special attention. Jesus know you need The Big Trip to See Inside the Dark, to see How All the Parts are Connected.

Jesus know White Boy got to have himself a Big Trip to Europe.

So that's just where he go. To where it all start. Angle Land.

Angle Land named for a Turk named Ing.

4.
White Man, He Cross Big Water

Fall in love. Read Wittgenstein. Walk those old clapboard streets knowing you're just like all the rest, what Americans forget. The English, the original "you're just like all the rest" people. No pointing out with the English, no, no. Fit right in. You're nothing special. You're barely even White. You're just here, with the rest of us, in the noose of history, waiting to be hanged.

White Man knows his potatoes and sausage. Knows his beer. Knows his women, short and to the point. Knows his punting, short and to the point, on small English rivers. Knows history is too huge to contemplate so contemplate women instead. Read more books. But they're no help. Books don't help to accommodate the enormity of it all. Books don't transgress enough, don't feel enough, or even if they do, they're not your transgressions and feelings.

Got to break rules.

White Man know how to break rules. Know he got to get inside of the rule so he can understand it so he can break it. Each rule made to be broken, so you can understand why it was there in the first place. So you can be on the other side of it, looking in.

Go to "The Continent," the only one that exists to the English, the one on the other side of The Sleeve:

Henry James wants White Man to be Complete, like Black Man want to be Correct. White Man, be you Complete? Got to Complete Your Education.

Go to Continent. See Big Land. Eat That Food. Fuck Those Women.

Get that Learnin

Learn good, for it shall be needful for you, in darker times still nearby, and bearing closer now...

White Man knows he took a wrong turn somewhere, go to Europe, fall in love, and go mad, but it all seems related, like it was meant to happen, like he, was Someone Special, granted a Special Audience, with the Divine Wisdom , set to percolate down into a Big White Book, like the Bible, except written on a Mac, but just as pompous and racist, but slightly less full of commandments, just as nonsensical, just as religious, just as devout, and musical, poetic, a real Group Feeling, a real Sense That This Belongs Here, this is Our Book, a Book For White People, though Other People Can Read it Too.

Yes, this is a Book For White People, but Other People Can Read it Too.

Or maybe I have it all wrong. Maybe it's a Book for No One At All.

Maybe This is Not a Book that Anyone is Capable of Reading, because it Should Not Have Been Written in the First Place, and so the best thing to do would be to Forget About it.

This is not a racist book. This is a true book. But maybe the truth is racist. Or maybe Americans are just obsessed with race and I'm being patriotic.

White Man, he go Uffizi. In that Florence. Big room, Big Art. White Man look it in the eye that statue. White Man know he small. White Man afraid. White man think: what it mean? Nobody know.

Go insane.

That evil spirit, he come in. Tell White Man: the world Make No Sense. Now, You Go Crazy, like a Good White Man.

Take off his clothes and run down the street. Get locked up.

Get taken away in the white van.

Nice old lady give him the shot.

Have strange dreams in the Italian Nut House, just like Stendhal.

Stendhal suffered from Stendhal Syndrome at the Uffizi Gallery, just like me, but it is jus another fancy name for what all black people know: The Crazy White Man Disease.

Crazy, what it mean? We know that one. Crazy make people say:

We no like you. You go now. You go way. Not wanted here. No good here. Go now. You go.

So you go. Go out there. See what goin on. Nothin good, but you see. See all those things which had been hidden, and for good reason. Things they write Bibles about.

Crazy, it a good thing. Like orange juice. Makes you wake up and say, mmmmmm.

We white people were a small people, ye future readers of history, and very ignorant. Like the Jews and Romans before us, whose bible we worshipped, we believed we were a Chosen People, Chosen By God, to rule over other races of the world, and that this was because we had Beaten the Winter, and had the right Phrenology on our Skulls, and Big Brains, and other lies, which informed us that all was right with the world, with God in his Heaven, and the King in his Throne, and the peasants in their trenches.

We were a small people but a good people, completely terrified of almost everything, from breakfast to the day of our death, but amused by it, because we knew that it was ultimately meaningless, or because we knew it all meant a great deal, but not to us, or because it meant a great deal to us but we could never know exactly what.

We white people were a very amusing people and very dangerous, because of our love for the Jewish / Roman Bible, which informed us (as did its antecedents which were monuments to the subjugation of their neighbors) that we were the natural overlords of the region, for made up "ethnic" reasons, involving our strong foremothers and forefathers who were "just a little bit better than all the rest." That crucial bit.

Jared Diamond did great service to humanity in his book *Guns, Germs and Steel* where he equates the improbable success of The White Man with simple geography; that those who chose to leave Africa and settle above the Sahara were statistically more likely to be "privy to the new shit," in the words of the Big Lebowski, and then rather statistically more likely to behave just like Mr. Lebowski himself, large and in charge, both humorous and humorless at once, and completely certain of the righteousness of his own destiny.

Yes, we white people know our destiny is righteous, but we are not quite sure why, and ultimately we do realize that we have simply been effectively brainwashed, that our Rulers of Yesteryear Effectively Planned this Out, knowing a large subjugated population was far more pliable if they believed they were Special.

So. White Man know now. He know he ain't really white. White just some genetic mutation ain't hardly mean nothing except insofar as it related to certain latitudes and certain dietary regimens, where you live and what you eat, nothing especially Special with a Capital S about that. Just normal.

I know, this Big Book of White be Very Ethnic, and so it be. It be devoted to an accurate description of My People, and so let it commence, if it has not already, with the Description.

Mother: large eyes, blue. A little squinty. A sneaky look to them, like she got the cream no one else has discovered yet.

Father: a moonscape face. The original Brain Child. A Nerd of the First Order, blessed with the singular blessing of being of Above Average Height, like his son. Unlike his son, he is sensible and does not write books, but is retired, and listens to music.

Maternal Grandfather: bombed the Japanese. Principal of a public Los Angeles high school until his retirement. Groomer of orange trees and builder of large model train cars, designed to contain other model train cars.

Maternal Grandmother: put upon but still capable of snarling when she felt like it. Able to be bullied into Monopoly by Our White Boy. Had the look of constantly hiding, from what, no one would ever be able to describe. Possibly an early victim of the Big Los Angeles Paranoia which Our White Boy would later encounter in earnest.

Paternal Grandfather: tall, aloof and very old. Died of throat cancer in the mid 1980s. According to family legend, tried to write a novel in a New York Hotel in the 1930s, at exactly the same time that Steinbeck was hammering away downstairs on *Grapes of Wrath*. My grandfather left early, having not written more than a page. Perhaps he left the typewriter behind. He did, eventually, write a book, which was published to more acclaim than this one will be, titled *On the Flip Side*, about his career as a record executive in Los Angeles.

Paternal Grandmother: the original cat. But not sure that she got her cream, and always wanting more of it. Polite enough to hide this desire, and charming enough to express this desire constantly in the form of amusing anecdotes that did not always make sense.

Both grandmothers eventually went mad. Both grandfathers stayed sane till death.

All in all a pretty picture of, if not upward mobility, then a good clean American vision of Working Hard to Stay More or Less Where You're At, a condition Alice of Wonderland would approve of.

We're still here. We're not going anywhere.

White Man returned from Italy, a changed man, and the same man. He know he crazy now. But he good at hiding it. Got himself a new American girlfriend because the English one was just as crazy as him, except about Jesus, and got himself a new job and a new a career, and then another new job and a new career, and then a new girlfriend, and then nothing.

An American success story. Cruising on the blood of innocents and our own ignorance, unable to stop.

But what is this, eh, a Marxist Liberal Claptrap? Didn't Our White Man Deserve His Own Success?

We know this story. We were a little better armed, and there were more of us, at the right times. Or maybe it's something else entirely. How can I know? History is not a satisfying answer, but it is the only answer.

White Man tired now. He go sleep. When he wake up, he tell more.

5.
Strong

White Man Book strong. He tell these things from love. Like James Baldwin. Or Steve Martin. Not funny like Steve Martin though. Not serious like James Baldwin. Crazy like White Man Book. Strong crazy, like the sramana, Santa Claus.

White Man Book will tell it like it is. Say what it know.

Maybe is no point. Maybe what White Man Book say everybody already know. This okay. There be worse things than too much book.

This White Man, he crazy. He think, I go Hollywood, get the big fame. Crazy talk. This same way grandfather think, back in 1920s era. He racist too. He write letter, in 1920s, back home to Brooklyn, say, "I help nice lady out, she no want to sit next to Chinaman, so I gentleman, I throw that dude out."

We don't say that word now. We say Chinese American. You know this. I know this. Grandpa not know this in 1920s.

But, what do the different word do? Many thing. These different word, many thing.

Many strange thing. Magic, like Gargamel.

You know the magic word for White Man, you

tell him. He want know them. So he can fly into the sky.

We already do that, he know.

But he want to fly too, like James Baldwin. Not gay like James Baldwin. Can't be black like James Baldwin neither. But brave like he.

Now, what we know about that nigger baby James talk about?

I know maybe what he about. Just that idea, that you want a slave. But if you want a slave, you the slave.

Now we know famous men. Maybe we talk about them some. Other things to talk about first though. Like this White Man.

He go Hollywood, that place, down here, in the Basin. Yes, fo washin. Get that brain hung out scrub real good, wash it up in that basin, and you be free, from all thought...

White Man not know what it about. Jews, they know. Arabs, they too. Russians, maybe. Ukrainians, them too. White Man not sure.

Not so sure.

But this is not Hollywood story. White Man he already write that one. This one about being White Man. Ethnic.

That different thing.

This different thing we hold inside, no danger, just dangerous, some thing like life.

What is it?

Love, maybe. Same as everyone got. But the flavor of love, that the ethnic part. What flavor you be. Same love, different taste. How do I taste? I not know.

Got to imagine it. In Texas, Friend Land, they say, "put on yo thinkin cap."

So I do.

Now I know, is not no point to a story not nothing happen in it. But plenty be happenin, you see.

This White Man, he sorry for the things that he did. But he not tell you about that part. He just tell you about the interesting part.

King White, he range over the land, in his mighty freedoms, got them hawks on his elbow, got that helmet on his head, he know he permitted, to ride over them kingdoms, let himself in any doar, jus go on in, and welcome himself, for he king, and this king, now elected in his White Skin, must make apparent to the people that he regal.

All that apparency just done broke us down. So apparent it flashed out our eyes.

I come Hollywood and it flashed me out, just like that. So bright it startle me, the deer, and that poor innocent Jewish family, not know how to stop. Run me down.

Is okay. Deer should be knowin better bout the freeway. Ain't no one say, come Hollywood, it free ride. No one say, come down here, we gots it living like kings.

Yes, that be why I write this book. Here in Hollywoodland, in this Wild West, we set the King to rest, in his berth, set out to sea.

For he done ride out over the land, one last time now, and we goan set him free.

Fly away now, fly away.

We burn yo ship and set you free, and then we be free of you too.

Now that we be riddin ourself of that King, King White, what do we be now? Ain't no democracy yet. No, just Money King, we know.

And by the way, pay that man, like I said. This good book here.

Well, maybe we be rid of that king too. I not know.

This the problem with that word ethnic. My computer here, he say, "ethnic" connected to ideas of "not us," from Greek times onward. Mean same thing, in the root, you know, as that Hebrew word "goy." You not a Jew, you goy.

You not us, you ethnic.

So I write this here book, like the Jews did that scroll of them. Now, this book not religious, you know that. It just White Man Book.

But like that Jew Scroll, this White Man Book has concerned itself real serious, in this not so serious way, with this ethnic thing.

Cause if I say, I ethnic, I be saying, I ain't you.

What is all these different flavors?

What one love did Jah be talking of, since as we can't see it yet? I not know. Not you either.

Our tribe, come from three other peoples, like

all tribes, that's all that 'tri' is, we not know either.

What is it, who is it.

Well, we goan have to do it for a while, is what I think. Is only way to make sense of it.

Why not.

This here be the ethnic tale of a white man, raised in the ethnic suburbs of Aurora, Colorado, and born in the ethnic mountains of Wyoming, which had been ethnically cleansed a few generations previous.

He know he a bad man. He know he not no good. But this book be good. Better than he be. Truer than. Maybe.

This here the tale of a white man, and how he came to be in America.

Some of you be sayin, I know, why this white man talk like dis. He makin fun of black people talk. No, is sheer jealousy. Imitation be flattery, you know. If I can not understand you talk, at least I can copy it. Then maybe I understand it. Okay then.

Once I was a child and I still am, not wondering why, just being, here south of Hollywood, in my freedom, not no one telling me what to do. And if freedom be good, we still want to give it to other people, even though some say that be a bad idea. But we know it a good one.

Come by here, and I got something for you. Something no man seen yet. This idea, like that Jewish Golem, walkin over the land, saying:

We here now.

Come by here. We know just what it is. I seen it. I seen it on the faces of these angry people here. Hard workin people knowin just what it is they do.

What is it now.

What come over you, huh?

Is all right.

There's nothing for it now, but to go on.

I goan take a break now. I be back.

White Man, he know. This be offensive this story, about a White Man. White Man he done tell his own story and everyone else their story so ain't no mo tellin from the White Man. He shut up now. White Man know.

You just tell yoself, this be one long shuttin' up. Just a little quiet before the Big Long Quiet in the sky.

Real quiet now:

Once, I be happy boy, in that dark little tower up the mountain, now I be the sad white man. Is funny story. White man think, one day he be rich be famous. Other people they think this. But maybe, de White Man he the best at it. He think, is my right. I got to be. This White Man, he know ain't like that, but still, some part of him think that. Oh well. He get over that one, like a truck to de head.

This truck to de head, it come over his head, because one day, he heard de voice of de Lord, just be talking in his brain.

Jus like Moses!

This terrible thing. De white man, he done read de bible so long, even if he ain't read the bible, he read the bible. Even if he ain't thought much about de bible it part of he thinkin. This how it is with de White Man.

He know, life go in America, he know, Science be strong, Science be where it's at, but deep down, Jeebus still be lookin around places, lookin to see, where he be at. Do White Man be sorry for what he done? Do White Man be sorry for thinking he da king?

Dis White Man, he know he ain't no king, he know America done be rid of dem and put in de new kings, of which he ain't one of dem either. He know is the right way to do things, American style. He know is useless to discuss it. He know all be right with the Earth and the rain, but deep down, he still be thinkin:

What if I special?

De White Man ain't special. We all special together. De White Man know that. But still he be thinkin, what if I be special in a different kind of way?

What if I can jus de mind-fuck the fuck out of de populace? This what de white man be thinkin. Just like Moses. So dis White Man, he go Hollywood, where all dem Mind Fuckers be at. See how they do. See what love be comin his way, like a freight train run over de head.

Dis White Man, he hear de voice in he head.

Voice say:

Yo, I be the Lord You God. Come Now, and be worshippin me.

The Stupid White Man, just like de Moses, he think, 'Yes, dis Big God he Notice Me, now I be doin what he say, so I be like de King.'

Dis Stupid White Man. He think, jus cause he be hearin de voice in he head, he special. What he doan know is: everybody and he cousin hear de voices in they head in Los Angeles. They just be ignore that shit. Everybody de Moses in LA. It ain't no special.

Dis White Man, he not know this yet.

So he do stupid shit, and get fucked good by The Man, not white or no color, just Man, behind the four walls, in jail.

No, he fortunate, no rape for him. Just metaphorical rape, of de mind.

Who the White Man be, I not know, but this White Man need tell his story now. It not a long story. You heard this kind before. White Man, go West. Tragedy.

Now, I did not encounter any Indians. They had been killed by my ancestors. When I come West, I encounter Californians. I was a Texas boy, you understand, raised if not born there, and we dress correct in Texas, like the Black Man do, except with different clothes. In Texas place, we wear cardigans. Not in California place.

White boy, he come West and he see all the pretty women, but they not see him. But we done tole this story already.

White Man go Europe, White Man Go Crazy, White Man Come Back, White Man This, White Man that.

Did the White Man really suffer?

Only in his crazy did he suffer.

No one be prejudiced against the white man because of the color of he skin. People like his color. White people, brown people, yellow people, they like his color. Red man, he not. But not many red man around.

And White Man know now, it not that they like his color. It just that they respect his color. Because his ancestors crazy, they kill you soon as look at you. Crazy.

This be the ethnic part of this story here.

White Man Crazy, it be Crazy different from other kinds of crazy.

Once upon a time, this White Man be homeless. And he meet a real nice old Black Man, he was a drooler, he talk with lots of spit in his mouth. This Black Man, he on the retirement, so he have lots of money in his pocket, money for the drink, for the chicken, and for go to Vegas when he want.

I know, this be stereotype story. But it true. I met this nice old man. He give me his vodka, I doan have to take it from him or nothin. Homeless people be nice to people.

This old Black Man, he crazy, but not like White People Crazy. He learn to tune out then Voices in da Head, and he just avoidin' the po-po, buyin his train ticket, sittin around, sip on the vodka, maybe pee himself if he a mind to, or walk around with his sleeping bag. He got a storage unit and everything. Keep his stuff there.

White boy, he happy to have a friend. Black Man, de Drooler, he know they ain't friends, but acquaintances. White boy not know anything but it okay. White boy on his best behavior.

Drooler so nice, he buy White Boy a phone, so he call his people. They try to call Drooler's people too, but they ain't around. White boy people, they around. They lookin for White Boy.

So he go into Mental Hospital.

White Man Crazy, it be dangerous. If you know it, you know they ask you: you ever hurt you self? Yes'm. You ever hurt the other people? No'm. Not yet anyway. That be later.

White Man: why he crazy? We doan know. Except, we got theory. It be: White Man he were Rich. Croesus Rich so rich. Rich make you crazy. That one theory.

Other theory: we not know. I like that theory.

I live now like Malcolm X, in the ethnic enclave of Koreatown, amongst the Koreans. They Koreans are very nice. They do not speak to you, we do not speak to them.

This not true. Koreans say hi when they old Korean man. Or when you give them money, then they smile. They like most people in this way.

In this ethnic enclave, I am the White Man you can spot a mile away, with the special Crazy in my head. The people here know, this White Man, he crazy, you stay away from him. This is how it be. It is okay like this.

When you Crazy, you alone. You make up your own friend, and talk to them. Sometimes, you even meet other Crazy Man, and be friends.

White Man, he drink his wine now. He sorry this White Man book done no good. He want it to be good. But he know is not ethnic enough. Even if he make it ethnic, it not ethnic. It only White Man Book. The book of all of us.

The White Man's story is the Story of All of Us. So history teaches. White Man, he come over the sea, with many struggle, such as slaves, and he see the Dangerous Land Afar, and he Conquer It. For it Dangerous.

Bring Many Gun, Germans and Steel with White Man, also Bibles, and lay this land to waste. Then, lay it to waste again, then, sell it to people. Then, steal it back from them. Then, sell it again. White man he clever this way.

This White Man he not clever like that. Texas boy they correct, got his they listen ears over his head, got his hand over he mouf, like teacher say, not say nothin.

Jus say Bluebonnet, Mockingbird, state flower, state tree. State bird, state flower. Bluebonnet story they teach go like this:

Indian girl, she love White Man. She love white man so much, she make little voodoo doll that she burn up like the White Man, spread he ashes on de slope, bring Big Rain, bring White Man, also Bluebonnet. The Bluebonnet Origin Myth, as taught in Texas public school 1980s time. True story.

White man, he know this bullshit but still has that pleasing feeling, like White Man Book here. You know you shouldn like, but you like. Why that be?

Is because of the White Man Crazy. Me, I seen different kinds of crazy, but there be no crazy like White Man Crazy.

Sometimes the White Man gets thoughts in his head. Like now. This thought be: why there be this White Man Book?

I doan know. Them Muslims, the Black Muslims, they doan know either. They say: Boko Haram. No Book for you. Maybe they know better.

Still, no crazy like White Man Crazy. You can put on the hijab, and dance the rain dance, but you still ain't crazy enough to conquer a whole continent and then lie about it.

Then again, maybe you is. Because White Man Story, he Everybody Story now.

Everybody a Nigger Baby now, Mr. Baldwin. Everybody want they a slave.

No, I know. White Man told a fib. Not everybody be a nigger baby, Mr. Baldwin. Only the White Man. No more nigger babies left except White Men. This why we so sad. No one will be nigger babies with us. Everyone think: this nigger shit, it for the birds.

White Man not think so, he still want to be the nigger baby. Why?

I not know.

Mr. Baldwin say:

These chillen, they no good at listen to mom and pops. (I paraphrasin here) But chillin, they good at turning into dem.

I look at dese quotations here, my Computer Man keeps them around, tell me all the thing Mr. Baldwin say. So many thing, he say. He done said so many thing I can't even believe.

So brave, Mr. Baldwin. So brave and so dead. So I got to be Mr. Baldwin now, even though I just a White Man with a big Crazy in my head.

Be like Mr. Baldwin. Say: see here now. I wise man. You listen.

I been in Koreatown here. Koreatown good town. You listen. Know like the White Man. Know like the Korea Man. Know like the Baldwin Man.

Mr. Baldwin, he say: (I paraphrase here), "these people, all the same. People write books, these people, all the same." Mr. Baldwin, he wise man. He know everybody like book. He know everybody crazy.

So what this thing, about White Man Crazy, Korea Man Crazy, Baldwin Man Crazy, everybody crazy right?

Not in this ethnic story. My crazy, it matter.

Those other crazy, I not know about.

The White Man fears hisself. So he design his society to keep hisself in prison, so he not have to look at hisself. If he see hisself, he go crazy. Bad crazy. Better to have the "good" crazy, keep you self lock up, not see nothing, then you never go bad crazy.

If you see something, especially in Los Angeles, you crazy, man. Nobody here saw nothin.

To know who you are, you got to know who else you be. You ain't just one thing.

My White Man, he know the long arc, not only of history but the universe, bending now. Bend now, white Man, reed in the mind, see not only Arrakis but the sandworm within it, you terrible blue eyed man, longing under your sea:

White Man know he no good. This okay. He somewhat good; in-between like. Neither hot, nor cold, but lukewarm, and so you can spit him out of your mouth, Bible say, though White Man hope you swallow instead, it sounds gross, but it's part of life.

White Man know he offensive son of a bitch, and this okay too. There worse things in life. Being offensive son of a bitch is useful to society. White Man remind you: White Man offensive. Hate the white man, is okay. We can take it. We tough like White Man. We know we okay. Not good, but okay. This is okay.

White Man. Get over you self. Is okay to be white. Is okay to be a man. We know this. Is no war against you.

Still, this ethnic novel, we know this. if any novel be ethnic, it be White Man Book.

Don't take my ethnic from me. Not yet.

White Man, how can you extract you experience, being only one White Man, and say it true fo de White Man?

I doan know, I do it.

White man, he got hold of me. Ain't no escapin him. Even if I wanted to I couldn't. Dis fever I be havin, done drug me unduh, in the black goo inside . . .

I know you me and I you, when we end, ain't no nothing but what you is, I is, but what here now in this between but us now talkin bout what we ain't too, ain't not yet, what we want be but not yet, take me home white man I tired, I tired today, take me home:

Ain't nothing else.

This idea home ain't nothing else but what it is, made up, the most needful thing imaginable, need it more than food, more than love, more than god, it home, the time before any other, like the womb:

I home but I know I leavin.

I leavin home, bruthuh, some come wit me, out in da dark, where the lions be, and I show you this thing I foun, when I just a boy, it light inside:

White man, he got the thing inside, this thing that Baldwin he have to, and Shakespeare, it god.
But what god know about black and white? Shel Silverstein, he say, god need he turn out da light, take away de black and white, so we all bruthuhs with no light.
And dis god inside he ain't go no light either but what he make.
So I make de white too.

I make de white and he make me, dis ting, ain't no nothing else, but the imagination too. I de nigger baby but I be other things too, Mr. Baldwin, I promise you man, I goan be so many thing, you see. You see, I promise.

Dis nigger baby thing, it complicato. If you is a nigger baby, if you is white, you be saying, I need dese races, cause I know, I at de top. So dis nigger baby, he de one at de top of de races. Nigger at de top.

Dis nigger baby at de top, he think that evolution end wit him, it like Adam and de Eve, dis end result, of de plan of de god.

6.

White

Man Brain?

White man understand the difference, this one, he done decided he smarter than other people. But he know this bad and good, ain't no escape from it. In de school dere in Texas they tell he: "you de brain."

De brain, de brain!

De brain, de brain!

Here come de brain!

Dis big mushroom sit on he back! Walk round wit him! Tell him: hey here, what this? And dis here, what dis? All dese question in dis mushroom on he back, de brain. Thinking: what I is?

What I is this man now sent to remind we, what we is, not yet, no not yet, summertime, I tell ye: I is now bent to your serf field make me you my melt my fever branch take me I hold it I build it this mark I make it take me, now wait describe and wait, the mind the arm and the reminder take to sleep to say dese things, terrible nigger baby, you barrier to de truth, you scion shrunk sent for to find dese tings we need but don't describe dem, no, ain't no need, just bring em in yo batch, catch dem and wait, you hold dem.

I hold dem, they with me, I promise.

Eggs or phantoms whoever, I got em, I tell ye: no one else. But I got em if you want em, these futures.

Dis white man, he demoted. He understand. He de wrong color. Old empire gone bye bye. Justice and the machination of justice, virum ex machina, come fore to hold this scale, tell who where when and why, and for how long.

How long we goan be nigger baby, Mistah Baldwin? Tell we. Tell we what we are.

But he dead now.

Same now as then, got to be better.

I know, is same.

White man, ain't not enough.

Tell de story, white man, tell how it be.

Dis comfort, it de problem. Beware of safety de man say, and he right. He right. Safe things they the prison, they the omen, of you church, of you lamp in de dark dat ain't goan reveal nothin but mo darkness, the womb.

Crawl out de womb, white man, be born.

Not to Jesus but only to de world, make it ye and make it whatever ye can, when you need, when you mark the time I mark it too, White Man, I goan tell ye:

"White Man, come ahead! White Man, come

here! Kumbaya white man and de chillin and de river goan needful tell ye what we wearin in dis wall past de border, over and up:

"Not de heaven, but de future. De future of de brotherhood, stranger now than ever, made new:

White man, he know de rules. Don't talk about White Man. Too many know about White Man already: he big, he strong, he racist, he a big murderer, and that is all he be. He ain't be nothin else!

No, that ain't true. He also be a whiny middle class ho, always talkin bout he be existentialist, he ain't no satisfied, even though he get everythin.

Yeah, this right. We be havin everythin, except what we want, which be power over our own destiny.

Same as you.

White man, he know the rules. Don't talk about dem rules. Jus be quiet. Shut up and listen. Don't talk, listen, White Man, shut you mouth.

Don't talk, listen, White Man, cause what you say might be so dangerous, you might just speak de truth . . .

Dis White Man know, he in the middle still, the overlooked middle child, same as the rest, middle hatin de middle, and de po hatin de middle, and de rich hatin de middle, jus as it supposed to be, take dat hate and chew it up good, swallow it and make it you own.

But this ain't de true story.

White just dat story cover up de other stories.

White Man, he like to write.

Why dis be?

Why all dese White Man writers?

I don't think it be only that de murderous arc of history, it leave only de white man wit de pen. It something else. Something racialist!

Some racialist poor-dumb obsession with de ink and de paper!

Makin dese marks!

Makin dese here White Man marks!

Yes, I say de writin, it be White!

Dis White Writin!

Out of Gobekli Tepe and strummin it madness into de breeze!

Out of de Gobekli Tepe into de breeze! Mad town! Mad White Gobekli Tepe town!

Dis old time religion!

Who died when! And why!

Dis be de record! Of our dey pilgrimages!

Dis be de record! Of our dey wars and de nonsense streams musical, dreams horrors beauties strumming on de guitar of orthographies immense subservient to de idea of de god, so many of dem we can not even speak, mumbling only, under the grave walls, what might come to be . . .

White Man Book, he know he ain't nothin. But

it he all he got, magnetic bumbler, strumbler true dirt and flesh, magic but only as good as he ideas...

What good an idea that two or more things at once?

What good an idea that be: even this idea ain't an idea, not whole, it need de others.

Yes, we goan move past de old time Gobekli Tepe religion, yes, we goan move past de old time philosophize and de old time de Writings of de Wise Men, yes, but:

What where we goin?

Was dere writin before dere was white?

Dis homeland idea, it de mos offensive idea der is. And de only idea der is, maybe.

But we know, we know, we need de big homeland, de whole of de Earth, make de room for everybody, we need it now, the rainbow nation.

White Man, he help bring de rainbow nation, we know.

We goan bring it.

But how? How if de White Man need his own book?

It okay.

White Man can have his book.

Write whatever you want.

Nobody care anyway.

This freedom.

Dis ain't no easy story, part because dem founding fathers, not de American ones, but de ancient ones, in Gobekli Tepe, dey want us forget we, who we be, cause better then, than knowing, what we become.

Like de black folks say, sometimes, they be forgettin, because it painful, just want to go on.

I go on but I go back too. Fucking time travel machine, dis.

Where dis white come from?

Now Malcolm X, he got hisself a theory from his brother man, cute cult leader black muslim character, say de white men were built by a crazy scientist along with the yellow man.

Now I doan know about the crazy scientist, but we do know after dem icebergs they melt, white skin come about, right 'long with agriculture, in Turkey, and China, right round the same time, spread by dem farmers, with they seed, from Gobekli Tepe, potbelly hill.

Gobekli Tepe, potbelly hill, come round and de worship, son, for we be don killin all dey animals and now we set in on de people.

De original lord's prayer, before Jews, before Sumer, was dere in Anatolia, for de wheat make us white, and we eat, we say, to da priest:

Priest man, give us dis day our daily bread, mon, and we eat it dis, so we grow white as the stars that we see through de soul holes, beneath de earth, where we bury our dead, and we eat it hey, we eat dat bread, white bread, white man, white bread, white man, de white bread of a white man, growing whiter, turning whiter, so too in Asia, from the estuaries of Hong Kong, spread over de land, the white, and de white, and wit de white, de state.

State of white.

De state of white.

White Man, he write book!

And dis book, it is so old, but maybe, just young enough, just young enough now, at 11,000 years, for us to change dis book, and say,

What is we doin here, hey? What mean god what bold munificent figure he come over us in dem soul holes, as we grew dem pot bellies and set ourselves over de earth, set ourselves as de lords of it, given dem bread and given dem penalties and all over dis earth, all over it, dis spread of de white.

Dis recent development.

Gobekli Tepe, to my eye, Anatolia, go east to my star and rise, for I attend thee on monuments of stone, no worry, no cry, only my blood, burning, for thee—

You crazy, you say. You say, dis not no story. You crazy. May be. May be not. May be you de crazy one. May be you not crazy hey enough just yet.

May be this White White Book is yo book too. Come over on your canoe, set to in your furrow, sayin, hey now, I got de plan, I got my eyes on de prize, of de galaxy.

White agency within you, mon, cane get you to obey dese lords so many year, hey?

You know what it is?

Not nor me. But I looking.

Come, look wit me, and see just where it is we be goin:

Los Angeles some else thing be born. Here in de west.

Young man.

I say, young man.

Hey, young man!

I got a direction for you to go in.

You know what it is?

Young man, you know what it be?

Where you goan go?

It be up.

Up to dem stars where be looking.

Some JPL motherfucker roun here.

White man!

You crazy!

Crazy man!

What you doin now!

Well, I be sitting here writin dis white man book. Thinkin, it make de sense now. We crazy, we.

Dese priests dey done drive us all nuts.

From out dat potbelly come all dis, all dis madness. Slavery and the rest of it. Slavery not only of de black man, but of Nature.

Tell me, Nature, what for we do now? Who we go to now, spaghetti monster?

Diana, help we. Great Spirit.

Come over de land and give us de sense we done somehow lost in these miracles of millennia defile us de brains, I not know how, but give us we dis chance, hey. Remake us, in some shape that we goan survive and so will else, hey?

Timaeus?

Father Time. You old nutter, tell us we, what we done. And tell us what for sure we goan do now, in this pas where done lost most everythin we thought we done made these so many years now. Father Time, what we now? What good is this white skin and this wheat cult now, hey?

What did it do to us?

Father Time, what did you do to us?

What for we know, and why, and what for we do, all dese ting, over the long goodbye of history, white father?

What for we do, so many horrendous thing, under this sun, that make us white?

What can I know, little white man, my only burden, just being a man.

Only burden being a man, the hardest one. After being at all.

Be at all.
Be now!

And so we done. What we want. Got that big story. Got that big temple.

These thousand monarchy, storm over us.

Dis White Man Book, just the little crease in its iron, made new.

Terrible thing, White Man Book.

Is violent thing.

Dis violence within me, what it be?

What shall I be, violent thing?

What for and what made?

What love and what hate?

What new and what old by me, is made?

What terrible thing.

What White Man is me, some old, some strange, some nurturing, terrible what white man is it! What turn and what face! What embrace is mine that I see, that I do.

Yes, dat old racist Kipling he knew it too. Jus like me. Dis violent wanderlust.

We got de word of de gods! Down in de hole in Potbelly Hill town!

Got de humus and de bread!

Got de story, honeychile.

Come right be and I tell ye, we goan be all over dis world . . .

Did you know, dem English people they named for Gobekli Tepe too? He he! Sho. Dat Ingvi he was King of de Turks!

Straight from Gobekli Tepe town to dem far cold aisles of ice!

What white man tale now, son? When we have carried the way for you, come over you and told you, it was necessary, and it was ours, and it could be ours, if we had it, if we made it, if we did it, so we did, and made you. Now what you gonna do?

Dese ancestors talkin now. Dese old white men...

White father, what for you did it? Did that thing there beside dat hill? That thing, wit de wheat...

It was necessary son. Same as now. Will you do the necessary thing?

What dat be, white father?

Kill, son. Go forth and kill.

No, daddy. Ain't goan do dat.

Then you will die, son.

Yes, we doan need dem spirits. We American-isch now. Ain't no spirits in Americanisch because dey so many spirits! So many spirits is like no spirits!

So many gods ain't none at de all!

Only my voice, carry me in this wind, ain't no one else.

No one else want to go where I go, not yet.

Just like Gobekli Tepe town. That terrible decision. Rock decision: to stop moving.

Now here, here in my voice, defend me, says that crazy first white man, he say, now herein, defend me, for my voice, it carry me, it wind me and carry me, I see it . . .

Well, he may say something.

But mostly, he just eaten dem wheat.

And lookin round . . .

For the young lassies and lads, over and over . . .

Then come Gilgamesh, then Jews, and it all over, white man, you done fucked up.

You done made it this thing, terrible thing, what you do?

Tell me, white man, what this be?

7.
White Man
Have a Thing

This white man thing, it for the birds. Ain't no purpose to it. Ain't no device. Ain't no hardly meaning at all. They say "blood will out" but I don't think that mean shit. Just this story.

This terrible little story.

Well, we goan get a new one. We know.

The Bullworth solution approacheth, same as the Alexander the Great solution, of fuckin!

But what about de writin, white man? What about de book part?

Well, what about it, white man? We all so proud, now, we know, look dis big book. Ain't no boko haram roun here, no, no, dis boko real good. Boko real good, kosher fidelis, yes, yes, gimme please!

Yes, we love the white book. But what is the book?

I was raised a young racist not knowing it, like all young white men of my country. Then we discovered what we were and could not bear it, and some of my race set to murdering, like our ancestors.

Other men, wiser than me, have no truck with any of it, regarding it wisely as a bunch of nonsense, since almost nothing is known under the sun, but the story of man and woman, and that one known hardly at all too . . .

But I be a storyteller and so cursed to care about the stories I hear, wanting to know, what they be, what they are, why they are, how they make me.

And in so obsessing, I give them so much power. This White Man Book control me, he make me white far more than those wheat berry seeds. Was not the seed so much as the word, eh?

Maybe. Maybe.

So what to do with this heritage, hey?

It's real good for killing but we done run out of people to kill. Or rather, they done got real tired of us our penchant for it, and come a calling, to say, "hmm, white man, put down dey guns!"

Yes, we know, goan put down dey guns.

We goan transmogrify this the killing instinct into civilized ways, just like our ancestors!

But what this be? Was it we was the best killers, or just the best bullshitters? Yes, just dem guns germs and steel, metal life and powder, come too hard, up the ass, and in the pocket, rocketing 10,000 years and more of the neolithic, into our tired red eyes . . .

Oh, white man. People tired of de story now. Give dem some rest. Let dem make up dey own mind hey? Don't be so jealous of the story.

What happened then?

Father, bearded.
Mother, bearded.
Uncle, bearded.
Father, bearded.
Mother, bearded.
The Earth.
Divorce.
A shrieking outlet.
Come to Texas.
Father shave the face.
Mother shave the face.
Uncle shave the face.
And I.

In Texas, we shave, like the Rasna, the original shaven ones, like the Brits, the original tattooed ones so all we'd need would be tattoos to be double original, clean shaven and marked . . .

In Texas there is infinity.

It is so huge.

Blood drunk in the land, and the oil money and the happy children.

And the loneliness of the wilderness, a wilderness that's both nature and the story of nature, fighting, fighting . . .

Teacher, bearded.

And teacher, bearded.

And little boy me, growin de beard, and he not know why.

De Principal, she a fine woman. She tell me, don't be telling those chillin you the boss. You jus let dem alone. Here now, read me do story. So I do.

When I done, I get to pick de special pencil erasers.

They send we divorce class. Feel sorry for we. Watch de film strips.

Learn about people who go away.

Little boy me, he thinking, what I is, that I got all these ideas in me head? Must be god.

Other chillin, they know, I just a nerd. They remind me by makin me cry. You jus a boy, not no god. Come now, grab de gun, and climb onto de lean-to, we goan ambush the other boys.

So I do.

White man know, he sorry. He sorry excuse. Ain't no more room for white man no more. He take up too much space. He dinosaur. White man he must be shrinkin, go into de hole. De rabbit dinosaur hole! Lay him de egg, wait out dis meteorite.

But white man, he need de mate. Ho ho ho.

Santa Claus not bring de stork too, you know.

White man gots to do de work like everybody else. He know.

On de playground, white boy know is better to be black than to be white. Black boys, they cool. This, though, only in de theory. In practice it something else.

White man know, them boys n girls, he think they uppity, they just watchful. Just like now. Watchin real careful. What the white man goan do?

What I do. I de SJW like de PCP, he angel dust, bring de message, of de revolution. Ain't no one want it, ain't no one need it, but I push it on ye.

Say hey, lookie here. Got some fine white crystal powder. Magicko! Get you real high. Change you whole universe?

First one, she free. And you won't be needin a second . . .

Easy to say. Easy to say, feminist, racist. Marxist, capitalist. All the ists, they good. Real strong. Got the big idea regimen, like the big drug regimen. Push it down they throat, say "ahhh." Me too. I sell lots of them bad boys.

But I know, it ain't the same. Ain't not the same now. Got another story we need to tell.

This ethnic story, what it be now?

What be the white man now? Who is the black man now?

Jared Diamond, he say there five races. Okay, fine then. But what about the others?

Judgin dese degrees of dissimilarity. You be real different from me, you be jellyfish, or de oak tree. Dis fine wit me. You do what you do, I do mine.

But you be like me. You be close to me. Then I real careful. I say: how you know you ain't me too? We goan find out.

Men they say: who is me? We goan find out.

War.
She war.
Like a blessing over the cosmos.
Cosmos, she mean clothes for the woman.
All this blood we goan soak her in.

White man know. Is not easy. But so many kinds of knowin that. Books, they good, but they comfortable. Ain't no exist them books till you got de time and de space, stretch you legs out. Ain't no philosophy without no full belly, we know.

Without big mouthfuls of bread, ain't no white to be had.

See, you want to talk about white and de black we gots to talk about religion too. Ain't no way out of it. Ain't no easy way to talk. Ain't no pretty story. Ain't no light at de end of this tunnel; this tunnel ain't have no end, man, she keep on going through.

Religion, she mean tied again. First by blood, second by language. Or maybe de other way around. Maybe the other way around, yeah. This what the Jews think; words come first.

Jared Diamond, he right that it geography.

Got placed on de map right.

So many mouths to feed.

She Gobekli Tepe, the original efficiency expert. This corporate America, she 12,000 years old, man!

She sayin: look here now. We done eat all dese animals! Too much eat de animal!

Now, we grow grain.

Could been any plant, man. Any old damn plant. Was the geography. Right smack dab in the middle. That where she is. Just a big damn crossroads of the whole human race.

Smart plant, she say, I like dese dem ape man crossin through here. They like me, maybe we get marry.

So we do.

Out of de water of light.

The miracle of the storage.

Granary.

Of ideas too.

Like magic.

Love.

She tell me: I love you, man. Come, give me some money.

So I do.

We goan burn through many a checking account fore we through this account.

This the thing here. We done get out of Africa. But she ain't done get out of us.

What we know in Africa? When we done crawl out of them trees?

One thing: we lonely. Real lonely out here. Friends they gone 'way. Out in the grass.

And then we knew: they's others out here too.

All dese others.

So many.

I say, why white man book even exist? Why she slay that part of me? Why she know not to do it? What tell her to? What she name there in the dark? Whose spirit come over and whisper these things?

How I know it ain't true?

She tell me: now, go. Go on. You ain't need me no more.

Maybe that what Africa tell us.

Go on. Go on now.

Like the man with the badge:

Keep movin'

We done got so good at movin we had to decide to stop.

Crawl into de ground.
Under the spell the earth.
Whisper:
I know her.
I know me too.

8.

White Man Belly

Potbelly hill, the original theocracy. '-cracy' she mean 'hard.' And that 'theo,' she mean 'holiday, festive, temple.'

Yeah, that Gokebli Tepe all right.

Is hard to be so happy all the time.

Without no animal friends. Done kilt em all.

Kilt all our friends. Eat em up.

White Man, she one long funeral.

So White Man Book, he just one of them sermons, over this stertorated corpse.

She done be a good woman to me, elk opossum hyena savage.

She done tell me all I know.

Now I kilt her.

She was a good lassy.

Done run all over the land.

Now she run in me.

White Man, he cannibal.
Eat all de friends.
So he know: what they be.
All them in me now.
And so dance, so sad now, to have the pot belly.

Cannibal!

Cannibal!

Cannibal!

Now you see: is question of geometry. We done run all out of places to go, there on Potbelly Hill. Run all dem animals down, run all them Neanderthals down, marry some, eat some, all gone.

Only the wheat left, and the hill, and a whole lot of animal bones.

Got to say: we draw the line.

Here, is my plot.

There, you plot.

The original Jews. Jews before Jews. Here my rock, she say:

I farm here.

You farm there.

Good lovin.'

Geometry. Before, we could draw circles. Sun, moon, tree, rock. Circle strong, she easy, she wise.

Other wisdom too:

In de straight lines. And de lines look straight

and maybe they ain't so.

She say, scientist, these lines they wave markers, in the fabric of reality.

This whole spacetime she one big mother geometry. Lines all around this sumbitch.

But why we got to kill everythin' to know, hmm? Why we go to know that way? Are all lines about killin?

Like a crosshair on de Earth. Sayin: here she be. I know who she is. One racist sumbitch.

But maybe I done got it all wrong. That likely too.

Me other SJW PCP pushers they know real good the story she can trump everythin, she wanna. Storyteller make anythin be true he want to say why. He got a reason to or even he ain't. Any evidence will do if she strong enough. If he wise enough. If he want it enough.

What this be?

This whiteness?

You know, this television joke, the cop he know who to arrest, look at the makeup bad, white, beige? Okay! Brown, black? Arrest.

Them wheat weren't no magic spell turn everyone one color.

She just this ingredient.

You eat her, then you need the white skin. No more vitamin K for her, 'lessen she come from the sun.

And we know, yeah yeah, go north, not so much sun.

So this whiteness is also the marker of: did you eat the wheat? And how far away did you go? She geometry too. Metric system of this little plant's travels. Wheat, she want to know: did you eat me? And how far you been with me? Do I know you from before?

So what this mean?

Do it mean: wheat, she coulda been anythin? We always goan kill each other no matter who, no matter how?

Well, yeah, is geography, geometry, we know. Where you at. Coulda been anything.

But it was this.

So the other part of the story, then, you see, she racist too.

'Cause the whiter you got, the stranger the story is.

But it geography too, we know. Just accident. England, Portugal, she close to the sea. She get first crack. With her guns and germs and steel.

But is this other thing, too, you see, not only the wheat, but what the wheat do.

What do she do, this wheat? What big magic she got over us?

Is the story, the story, brother. Whatever you want it to be. What do you want wheat to be? You want her to be magic, or just some plant? You want her to be a demon, an angel, or both or neither? You want to blame the wheat for all these evils humans be done?

With wheat, see, come the state. Come the state religion. A story more and more agree on. Don't matter if it true or not. Just matter if it make sense.

White, she make sense.

Eat our grain, this day, no trespassing here folks, but only some forgiveness, in each wheat bushel, and we know: who we are.

This little genetic marker in the geometry of spacetime.

Easy way to tell:

You been puttin in yo time, Chicken Little?

You done plowed and furrowed and prayed? Or you only be shoutin how de sky, she fallin?

Yeah, this White Man Burden, she farmer burden. The burden of the terrible success this killin and geometry.

This White Man Book, this the new shit. De plans of de grain and de temple. The same thing.

Every White Man Book, she worship both those things.

But one other thing:

Now we know, that Neanderthal, he white too.
How that Neanderthal get to be white?
Was it wheat?

What do it mean? We not know.
But what do it mean now? Rainbow nation she comin, but the metaphor, she ain't right.
Not the color of you skin, but the content of you character.
But that ain't the world we live in.
What rainbow of character, who she be, and how she fly, over our they houses, making our truth, stronger together?

White man, he got the illusion of normal.
He got the illusion, everything okay.
He believe, things, they get better.
He believe, this what God wants, or maybe, this what Science wants, or maybe, this what I want, and what everyone want, so it happen.
But it not happen yet. Not yet.
White man, he believe, I work hard, I get rich.
No more.
No more white man belief.
No more white man believe power over others make him powerful. Not this white man.
But I got to be the black man now, you see?
Got to work twice as hard, just to show you, I ain't relying on the color of my skin, or rather, just like the black man, that I can do the job just as well.

Got to shout twice as loud, just to be heard.
Maybe.

This question of white, it question of masses of
population. Without the many many, they ain't no
white.

White, it invention of the many many. A management question.

All these hey people. What to do.

I know, new god. Big Man in de sky.

I know, new temple, rape you chillin.

I know, get me de overseer, make you work.

Only now, now, 12,000 years later, we got dey
robot.

De white man state, it no need dat God in de
sky now. It no need no rapin' temples. It just need
de robot.

And you know what robot mean. It mean
"slave."

It a question of consciousness too. Pharaoh, he
ask: is my Jew a person?

Descartes, he ask: is my dog real alive?

Slaver, he say: slave, he ain't real feel dat pain.

Now dese robots here, who they be?

I not know. But they a management question
too. This strange white man magic.

Terrible magic of de pharaoh.

Yes. Pharaoh, he mean "Great House."

Economy, she mean, "household management."

How we manage this great house now.

All these big homies done fill out de place.

Well, you tell me.

Maybe now, they White Man story, he make sense. Cause we done get so good at killin, we get the lonely, had to talk about how to make these corpses get up and they walk.

Jesus and Lazarus and Frankenstein's man alive, little Gobekli Tepe stories, little mongrel golems to keep us warm, in the hot savannah sun, now that we done kilt em all.

Done come back now, hear? We goan make new friends. Else we perish.

Dis de story of de White Man. But it de story of you too, whoever you be. White woman, Black man, Yellow woman, whoever, this your story too.

Cause White Man, he ain't nothin, but this management question.

De white, it just this mantra, sayin: we be many. Got to get smart now.

And de funny thing, part of getting the smart is getting stupid.

Getting more friendly, less intelligent. All these bodies, got to make friends. Get smaller brain now, but friendly brain. Less aggressive brain.

This the story of wheat and white too. Progression. Civilize dese bodies.

But where we draw the line, man?

Can we get too civilized?

Can we get too white?

White man, he crazy. We know. Why? We not know. Or maybe we not sure yet.

How he crazy? He hear de voices in de head. In this, he same any other man, but something different. What different? He got de infrastructure, magnify that signal. Who know?

White man, he go West, come Hollywood, hear de big voice in de sky, say, "you famous, big picture man." Same as ten thousand others, hear dis voice.

Den Hollywood beat white man up, tell he, you stupid, now you no money. Go jail, no $200 for you. This our $200. Bye bye. Same anyone else.

White man, he say. White man say, this not fair, he sue the court, tell the judge, not right. Judge take another $200 from de white man, say, it fair now.

Justice be served.

White man say, funny. Funny time, this Hollywoodland. Good sense of humor these Jews have. Gobekli Tepe done taught them good. Better than me.

White man say, I know, I be teacher. I have de degree. Educate these sumbitches. Learn them the readin and de writin. Learn de self too.

Gobekli Tepe say, these diverse times now. White man no more. You go elsewhere now. Go try de Skid Row. White man make good heroin addict, maybe. Funny.

Why dis white man so crazy?

Why he believe Enlightenment? Why he think dis big voice in his head like de Moses some special thing?

Boko not haram for him, but why?

Here in boko, de word. De word, he say many thing. Say, this may be a thing. This other, maybe not. Which he exist, which he not exist.

Boko he say, now, which you want?

Which you want, white man, black man, yellow man, white yellow brown woman, which you want ape? Which sand door temple or flyway you got in yo head, tell we, and we goan make that sumbitch come here to town, in de words you say.

It ain't no god in de head. It we. Big we now, maybe not no rainbow, but whole lot of burn sienna and shit. De burnt field of de land come home to roost, on all our earth tone skin.

We make de vitamin K from de sun, ain't no need eat no animal. But still we do.

Which world you want, white man? Tell me, and we make it so, Piccard Skywalker shit. De words de ensign engine goan trample de fabric of reality for we, if only you say.

Word, flesh, is all de same shit. Got to cooperate.

Still, this ethnic question, it so dangerous hey? This ethnic boko. We say, white, he this management question, some accident de geometryo. This white thing, it both the ultimate ethnic, say, we de king now bitch, but it also this end of the ethnic, say, we de crossroads, got de management questions, we goan turn that bitch into some useful.

Dis white, is it a wall, or a gate?

Mus be both.

9.
White Man, He Dig

White Man, he know the way. Right under Big White House. Come, dig with me, see what we find. Find all kind of thing.

See here, this Jerusalem. And see here, this Memory. And here slavery be, and money. Digging under the house.

White Man House is bold! Shaking under the sun! Stake careful wall and people moving under light, their loads infinite like the gods!

White Man House he strong, he move under the light too, like a tipi, tipping down into the crater of his thoughts:

White Man House move under the light and he say, "be healed," "my blood shall heal thee," cause he think he god too. Crazy White Man.

Dig my honey and I show you my barrel of nickels, burned from the cross. I bought every one, with my soul.

Here the White Man knows his innocence, for

he can forget anything, if he work hard enough.

White Man know better to bury than to remember.

This White Man Book poetry. You sing it. Like the sharecropper sing. This a song to god, asking: why, God?

Why you make us Crazy White Man like this?

This Crazy White Man: what use he now?
Done used up his time, maybe.
Maybe. Maybe not.

Blast off into yo Space

Faire des menages, White Man, in this Big White House, do the housework like you should, scrub all they gods and make em shine, with the wine beneath, in de basement. Faire des menages, and sing while you do. Manage real well, now. This house goan be a ticket into space—

If I tell you everything you need, White Man, where would the fun in that be?

Didn't Mr. Baldwin know, part of the fun be in telling you we know something you ain't yet?

Come on White Man, what you think you figure out? Baby in you sleep. Dream, dream with me, White Man, and I fo sure tell you something you need to hear: hear well, and hear it for it fo you chillin too; this fire from the sky she come again, and you house goan blast off into the space, but afore that happen you need this:

White Man, he dreamin. Of a better world. Some say, one without he in it. That peaceable kingdom for shoar, drummin round he house, makin its rude music, to show him what they be.

We who know what yo dream be, be waitin, for you wake up:

Wake up, White Man.
White Man! Time fo dinner!

No wheat for you, white man. We animal to-night. Eat the red sleep of the monkey meat, when you remember all the thing you thought you only dream of; it real; know the taste and the stomach of you ancestors, afore you house rise over the land, afore no pillar comin round to dust, this the long way out White Man, kin you see it afore you blast off?

Come here, White Man, and let me show you: this dust of you sleep, and the summer of the land, underneath you feet. What made it hurt you? What harm it do you? What nature creep under you soul, to try to keep you out?

All these creatures do you right, you let em. Only let em, White Man. White God. Slaver man.

We slave you too, you know. With all we right dignity and shame. All that wisdom not lost, White Man. You jus forget.

Come out that pillar o salt, white boy. Ain't nothin here to hurt you. Only de sun.

Yeah, that sun hurt, we know. Why you think youse black before? Before that mountain done start shoutin at thee. Come here, White Man, nigger baby be done taught a lesson now:

Each bite you eat, it say:
I you
I you too, White Man

Heed the White Man within, for he shall show you music, not of the jungle nor the savannah, but the deep above, lighting and shallow ruse for the knowful door out and gone; spacetime unravels for thee, though you be not the first, and it shall keep thee needful if you only let it.

Be needful, and rise low over this you dawn, if you would stay a while and meet all these creatures of the Earth, afore you done.

They need you too.

I dream of the shallow thing you be, lying beneath, under the long rose and hurtful dawn, sun mercury and stone, where you still cryin baby, wandering, where momma gone?

Where momma now, White Man, after you gone beneath through yo soul holes?

I see yo shallow thing and I done wring it out, for the laundry.

Scrub you good, White Man!

I scrub you so good! I scrub every last thing you are!

Under the dawn and music! I done drum out you soul! And I still do it! With every breath you take!

Under you stone. Over you head.

We gone crazy too, you know. Over everything you did.

From Gobekli Tepe town come needful thing so many, radiation extreme, the long regard of the radio, and the ratio of the medulla and the scissor and the weeping creep oer you stones marking territory not on soil but inside:

How much you worth now White Man? How much it reckon you now? Have you even reckon this world much? Let it take you down, and show you, how to eat:

Eat up. We got talkin to do yet. Afore I show you you lesson.

Show me where it hurt, now. I goan make it hurt more.

You reckon this Earth much now! Right now! You reckon this Earth.

10.
White Man Will Work

About da time. Time fo many things. If'n I tell you what we need, ain't no guarantee. Better maybe I don't tell you nothin' mo now, jus' hole on to the ghost of da thing, make it sing.

White Man suspect things mean things. Why he know? Why this or dat?

De ghos' tell him. Shinin' American Ghost.

Here in de lan' where we goan lose black n white de quickest. If'n we can.

Clear the river of de moss. Set roun it with you hands these wood, make it straight with de rock, so the fishes can sleep there, and be dreamin there, and we goan fish 'em.

Make the river next to the rock, fo us to sing at, and for any boats you be wantin'. I no like boats but you like whatever please you.

Over here, make de musical bandstand.

And over here, a chalkboard for de chillin.

We kin grow wine here. Grow asparagus. Grow collard greens and taters and mos' everythin' needful for us, if'n you want it enough, you kin make this shining river our own, wherever it be.

But de ghos say this:

"I am de ghos," he say.

Yeah we know. So what else.

"I am come with a message."

Yeah we know. So come on.

"What river pleases you also pleases me, if you say my name in the dark. Come be with me, and I will show you the long drunkard of midnight, after his storm is passed, and the deeper urgency of the dawn, shining over the light, and within it, for you to pray at, for you to shout in, and dream. But if I please you you must also please me, for I am a river, and I run from mountains to sea, both places you have been many times and worship, but now, with your Great White Kingdom you could bring both things low, mountain and sea, and so poison me. It's nothing to me, for in the infinite stretch of my time I cannot really be poisoned, but I can poison you. And what nourishes me, more than any other food, is hate."

Dig ghos be so angry. He chill my bone. Go on now, ghos'. You go on now. But he won't, he still speakin'

"I can pool by the child's feet. And by the man's. I can run around your legs. Around the legs of the dog. The king's legs are mine too, to wind around, and the voices of your children carry through me faster than through the sky, to infinite lands I keep inside. I move over your village and through it, inside the name of your children. I am all your gods, infinite and various, and I am king too, in my way, watery and deep, shallow too, and made musical by the earth. I care not for you in any ultimate way, but only that you are here with me, and have been made known to me with your feet, and your eyes. If you come with me, I will teach you so many things. I have taught you them before. Some of them you have forgotten. Some of them you are remembering. If'n I teach you that, will you come with me, into the sea's deep, and sing my name, where I am reborn?"

White Man he set to work, not on White Man Book any longer but some other kingdom stretchin' his eyes up for to look again, always lookin' round, askin': "what mine now?" "And what mine now?"

Everything be yours, White Man, and nothing be, cause we done find out, what you did.

Come here now, chile, and listen to the sound of the deep:

II.

White Man Can Listen

I am listening. But I do it with fists.

Do I fight against myself? Very well, I fight against myself. I am small, I contain only a small piece, of revolution.

The revolution lives inside you.

The revolution lives inside you.

The revolution, it lives inside you, but not always when you want, not always when it is convenient, not always when it seems logical, appropriate and sane, not always when its aims are exactly yours, not always when its goals are clear and reasonably attainable, not always when its soldiers are without sin, without selfish motives, without small kings and queens, lurking dangerously within them.

I listen with my fists in front of my body, over the keyboard and clutching my phone. I white man, manager, terrible manager of these 12,000 years of white, to know just how we can become better, more American, if American can still mean the great experimenter, the foundation of all science, to see just what it is that works.

Work with me, and be healed, not of injury or fatality, not of grief or pain or heartache or memory or shadow or hate or fear but only of meaninglessness. Mean with me; be mean with me. Our meanness shall transcend the world; it shall remake it. It shall root up New York, London, Paris and Abu Dhabi, Baghdad and Istanbul, Beijing and Sao Paulo. It shall smash idols, not in the mountains or in temples, but in the mind.

Like the insane Mormons, we shall become saints, which is only to say, we shall remember that we have power, and are willing to exercise it, and set ourselves apart from other men and women only for as long as it takes for them to join us, and see inside this terrible heartache of history, and how to reshape its course.

White Man, he kill, for he learn just how good it be to kill, why he do it, where and how. White Man, he study killin for it his religion, of blood.

In our be blood religion, we got fire in dey soul, made new and old, inside our hands. Inside our dey brains. Inside our willful dreams.

But how hey shall we know, which boundary be the one we need? Which dem bounry Jew stones, and de Achaemenid ones 'fore dat, shall we be settin in de ground to know, de ground of de mind to know, who dey enemies of we revolution?

Who dey enemies, hey?

You be my enemy?

You be my fren?

I mus know, you tell me it, and I listen. I listen with mey fists, and with mey heart.

Reach down, and in, along they spinal cord, along that long road of sin, chordata dreamer, made dey flesh, oxygen breather, runner wistful 'fraid and mellow like de sea, reach down and in, and take hold, of that deeper self, who breathes 'gainst you face like rain, and tell him, or her, jus' who you be now.

Be new again, under de white and de brown de yellow and red skin be new again, under every trap a revelation, this sky be one but we drummin it faster now, we ain't even know, and I be wonderin, jus who I be too, like you.

Tell me: I want know.

Tell me: who is it now?

Who we be now, White Man?

Terrible pull of the Earth.

My brother.

Ah bum bum may bum, may bum bum ay bum. May bum bum bay be bum dow, bum hey dee dow,

bum dow.
Bum.
Bum.
I be bum!
I be bum de dum!
I be de dum bum!
I be dum bum dum bum dum bum!
Day bum bum bum bum bum.

White Man, he terrible thing. This dream he hold over dey stars and dey lan'. De lan', it know him. It make him. They say, humanity be dis ting, dis terrible ting, that Nature be doin.

You be done?

You be bein done?

I doan know. I doan know, jus what it mean.

Maybe, but we do it too. Ain't slaves yet. No more slavery America way. Not yet.

Dis terrible thing, de Thing from Rejkjavik to Gobekli Tepe, Anatolia to my eye, its terror mus still be described.

So let us describe.

De White Man Fear.

De White Man Fear it is like dis: we fear de miscegenation, for we be fools, and having come across this terrible convenient mechanism of determining outsider from within, like Jews and their shtetls, we done decide some time ago endogamy be this thing we be preferrin. So we say.

Like Tay-Sachs for the Jews, White Men be

comin on the revelation of how stupid we.

Wheat done make us dumb; nothin for it now but to enact the Bullworth Solution, who done come anyway, over every beach, road and soil, over every woman's hearth, needful romantic and full of bliss, that union of us dey cousins like all millennia come across dey mountains with they seed.

We shall know it too; ain't no disaster but what we make it. Bullworth was a racist asshole with Big Jews on his schedule but he know the truth too, of the bedroom and the soul.

The soul be washed clean in the bedroom, maybe. Or maybe it never needed to be clean to begin with.

De White Man Fear is like this: dis philosophical question. Same as any thing alive on dis Earth.

Why I be White?

And why I defend it?

I be de nigger baby, okay, I know now. And I not know what mean the dissolution of de slaver within, I not smart enough fo dat. Maybe Mr. Baldwin he tell we an I miss it, I not know.

All I know is I got my story now. It dis White Man Book. It white on the cover. And on the inside, dese little black lines. Like DNA spirals. You can move em around if you want. I not stop you.

De lines, dey beautiful. More beautiful than the white.

For they shape the cosmos, who only mean: the woman dress.

About the author

Robin Wyatt Dunn was born in Wyoming in 1979. He writes and teaches in Los Angeles.